Sleeping Beauty

Retold by Heather Amery

Illustrated by Stephen Cartwright

Lang

There's a little yellow duck to find on every page.

This is a good, kind King and his Queen.

After many years, the Queen has a baby girl. The King and Queen are delighted, and love the little Princess.

The baby Princess is christened.

Six good fairies come to the feast at the palace. The King forgets to invite the seventh fairy, who is nasty and wicked.

Five good fairies make good wishes for the baby.

The sixth good fairy is just about to make her wish. Then, suddenly, the wicked fairy appears, looking very angry.

"She'll prick her finger on a spinning wheel."

"Then she'll die," she says. "No," says the good fairy. "My wish is she won't die, but will sleep for a hundred years."

The Queen cries and the King shouts.

"All spinning wheels in my kingdom must be burned," he orders. "Then the Princess can't prick her finger on one."

When she grows up the Princess has a Grand Ball.

It's her seventeenth birthday. The six good fairies come
to the palace. Everyone has forgotten the wicked fairy.

The next day, the Princess finds a little staircase.

She has never seen it before. In a room at the top is an old woman, with a spinning wheel. It's the wicked fairy in disguise.

"What are you doing?" asks the Princess.

"I'm spinning. Come, I'll show you," says the old woman. The
Princess puts out her hand and pricks her finger.

At once, she falls fast asleep.

Everyone else in the palace goes to sleep too. The six good
fairies carry the Princess to her bed. The wicked fairy disappears.

Nothing moves in the palace for a hundred years.

Outside, a thick forest grows up around it. Only the roof shows above the tree tops. The good fairies watch over the palace.

Then a young Prince walks near the palace.

He sees the roof and asks an old man about it.

"A Princess sleeps in there," he says, "but there's no way in."

The Prince walks to the palace.

The trees move apart and let him through. He runs up
the steps and in through the open door. It is very quiet.

The Prince finds the Princess asleep.

She is so beautiful, he kisses her very gently. She opens her eyes and smiles. "You've come at last," she says.

Everyone in the palace wakes up.

"I'm hungry," says the King. "Tonight we'll have a great feast," and he thanks the Prince for saving them.

The Prince asks if he may marry the Princess.

"Of course," says the King. "Yes, please," says the Princess.
Soon there's a grand wedding, and they're always happy.